OTHER CREEPIES FOR YOU TO ENJOY ARE:
The Ankle Grabber
Scare Yourself to Sleep
The Flat Man

For Elinor (RI)

For Graham (MK)

Text © 1988 Rose Impey
Illustrations © 1988 Moira Kemp
This edition designed by Douglas Martin.

This edition published in the United States of America in 2004 by
Gingham Dog Press
an imprint of School Specialty Children's Publishing,
a member of the School Specialty Family
8720 Orion Place, 2nd Floor, Columbus, OH 43240-2111

www.ChildrensSpecialty.com

Library of Congress Cataloging-in-Publication Data is on file with the publisher.

This edition first published in the UK in 2003 by Mathew Price Limited.

ISBN 0-7696-3365-X
Printed in China.

1 2 3 4 5 6 7 8 9 10 MP 08 07 06 05 04

Jumble Joan

By Rose Impey
Illustrated by Moira Kemp

GINGHAM DOG
PRESS

Columbus, Ohio

There is a dark and dusty attic
in my grandma's house.
I never go there on my own.
But one day,
my friend Mick and I
decided to take my little sister
there to scare her.
It was all Mick's idea.

After dinner,
while Grandma was taking a nap,
we led my sister up the stairs.

At the top, I whispered,
"Are you sure that you
   want to go in?"
Mick answered,
"I am sure if you are sure."

So, I turned the handle, and
the door creaked open.
We tiptoed in.

The attic was full of old things that
were packed in boxes and bags.
Piles of stuff covered the floor.
A tall, brown rocking horse
stood in the middle of the room.
It had big teeth and
staring eyes.

"Should we ride it?" I asked
   and winked at Mick.
   Mick said,
"Oh, I wouldn't
   if I were you.
   It looks like it is
   one of those
   Ten O'Clock Horses."

"Ten O'Clock Horses?" I asked.
Mick said, "At night,
when it is dark
and you cannot fall asleep,
listen very carefully.
When the clock strikes ten,
you will hear the gallop
of horses' hooves."

"Close your eyes
   and do not peak.
   If you do, you will see
   the Ten O'Clock Horses
   breathing on your window,
   watching you."

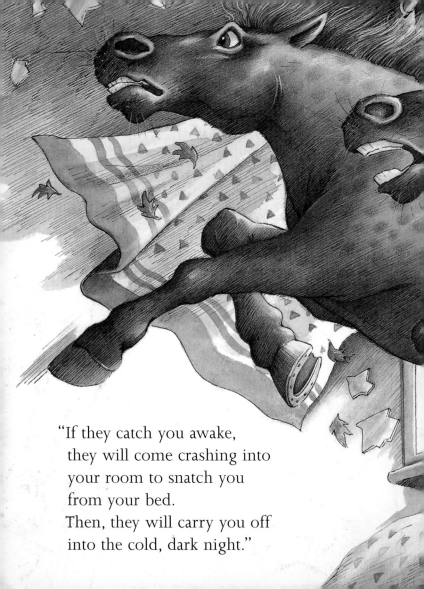

"If they catch you awake,
   they will come crashing into
   your room to snatch you
   from your bed.
   Then, they will carry you off
   into the cold, dark night."

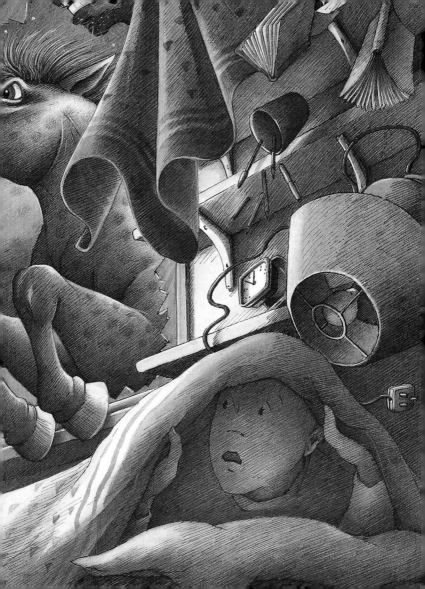

As we stood looking
at the rocking horse
with the staring eyes,
it suddenly rose into the air.
Then, it came crashing down.
Its mouth was wide open,
ready to bite us.
Mick and I jumped
out of the way
just in time.

"Get away from there," I told my sister.
"Do you want the horse to bite you?"
Sometimes, she is lucky that I am here
to look after her.

Next, Mick spotted a huge cage
that was covered with a cloth.
It looked as if something
were sleeping inside,
not wanting to be disturbed.

"You'd better stay away from there," I said,
"or else!"
"Or else what?" asked Mick.
"Or else the Deadly Vampire Bat
  may get you."

"Deadly Vampire Bat?" asked Mick.
"Yes," I said. "For over a hundred years,
  it has lived in that cage.
  As long as it is kept
  in complete darkness,
  it is harmless."

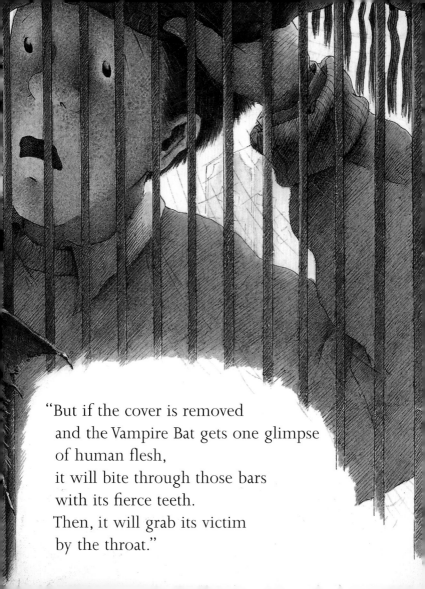

"But if the cover is removed
and the Vampire Bat gets one glimpse
of human flesh,
it will bite through those bars
with its fierce teeth.
Then, it will grab its victim
by the throat."

Mick was suspicious,
but I could see him
watching the cage,
just in case it moved.
Then, it did!
It started to shake,
as if something inside
were waking up.

Slowly, the cover began
to slip off the cage.
Mick and I backed away,
bumping into one another.

We started to scream.
But then we stopped.
We don't scare that easily.

It was only a stuffed parrot
that was full of moth holes.
Mick and I didn't think it was funny,
but my sister laughed.

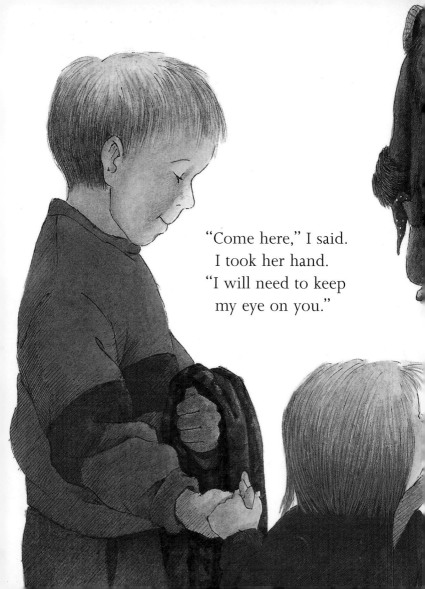

"Come here," I said.
I took her hand.
"I will need to keep
my eye on you."

It was too late, though.
My sister had spotted the closet.
She wanted to play dress-up.
Mick soon put a stop to that.
"You'd better watch out," he said,
"or Jumble Joan may get you."

"Jumble Joan?" I asked.
　Mick winked at me.
"She is a horrible old woman,
　who kidnaps little children," he said.
"Little girls mostly," I said,
　"with light-colored hair and blue eyes."

"She waits in dark cupboards
    and deep closets," said Mick.
"She hides in attics," I said,
"pretending to be nothing
    but a pile of old clothes.

"When it is quiet
   and starting to get dark,
   she stands up
   on her big, rubbery legs
   and wobbles out,
   searching for
   little girls to steal."

"When you least expect it," I said,
"she shuffles up behind you,
   drops to the floor,
   and lies there without moving."

"Little by little," said Mick,
"she edges herself
  closer and closer.
  Then, quick as a flash,
  she grabs you
  and stuffs you
  inside her great big skirt."

"No matter how loud you scream," I said,
"no one will hear you.
  You will be trapped.
  She will carry you, struggling,
  back to her cold, dark den."

It was chilly in the attic now.
The wind was blowing in
through the skylight.
It was getting dark.

The clothes that hung from the closet door
began to rustle and move.
The empty arms of the coats
seemed to be moving toward us.
Mick and I looked at each other.
We didn't say anything.
Very slowly, we began to move.

Right behind us,
in the middle of the floor,
was a huge pile of clothes.
It lay there soft and lumpy,
blocking our way to the door.
"Mick," I whispered, pointing.
Mick nodded.

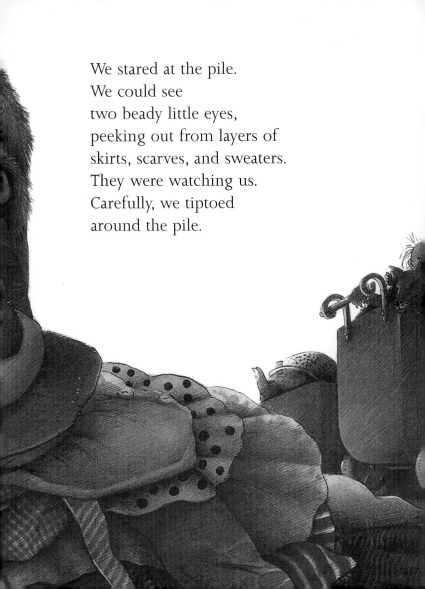

We stared at the pile.
We could see
two beady little eyes,
peeking out from layers of
skirts, scarves, and sweaters.
They were watching us.
Carefully, we tiptoed
around the pile.

We were almost to the door,
and Mick reached out
for the handle.
Suddenly, the mountain of clothes
rose up, rushed forward,
and tried to grab us.

"Gotcha!" it said.

Mick and I didn't
waste a second.
We ran out the door
and down the stairs
as fast as we could.
We didn't even wait
for my sister.

"She can take care of herself!" I said.